Penelope

Lively

Lost Dog and Other Stories

PENGUIN BOOKS

PENGUIN BOOKS

Published by the Penguin Group
Penguin Books Ltd, 27 Wrights Lane, London W8 5TZ, England
Penguin Books USA Inc., 375 Hudson Street, New York, New York 10014, USA
Penguin Books Australia Ltd, Ringwood, Victoria, Australia
Penguin Books Canada Ltd, 10 Alcorn Avenue, Toronto, Ontario, Canada M4V 3B2
Penguin Books (NZ) Ltd, 182–190 Wairau Road, Auckland 10, New Zealand

Penguin Books Ltd, Registered Offices: Harmondsworth, Middlesex, England

First published in *A House Inside Out* by André Deutsch 1987
Published in Puffin Books 1989

This collection published in Penguin Books 1996
1 3 5 7 9 10 8 6 4 2

Set in 11.5/13pt Bembo Monotype
Typeset by Datix International Limited, Bungay, Suffolk
Printed in England by Clays Ltd, St Ives plc

Contents

Lost Dog

DOGS are odd. They are animals, no doubt about that; but to other animals they often seem like off-shoots of human beings. This was certainly true of the dog at Fifty-four Pavilion Road, a rough-haired white terrier called Willie. The other creatures in the house thought Willie a helpless fellow because he depended on the Dixon family for food and a roof over his head. Mind, in the case of the mice this could have been said of them also, but I suppose they would have retorted that at least they risked life and limb to get their meals whereas Willie had his handed to him in a bowl. But the real difference is one of outlook rather than the getting of food and shelter. Dogs tend to take a human point of view; they even behave, up to a point, like people.

Willie loved Mrs Dixon. In fact, he didn't just love Mrs Dixon – he adored and worshipped her. He was polite to the rest of the family, but it was Mrs Dixon who was the centre of his world. He had a healthy respect for Mr Dixon, and he put up with the children – Julie who was nine and Andy who was seven. He had rather mixed feelings about the baby, since he was jealous of him and suspected (rightly,

I'm afraid) that Mrs Dixon loved the baby more than she loved him. But most of Willie's time was spent trailing around after Mrs Dixon, moping if she wasn't there, and admiring her when she was. He would sit in the kitchen, or the sitting room or wherever she happened to be and croon to her in dog language which of course Mrs Dixon neither heard nor understood.

'Oh, you are so beautiful,' he would sing, 'you are so beautiful and so wise and so clever. There is no one like you. I will do anything for you. You are the sun and the moon and I want to live all by myself with you for ever and ever . . .'

It was just as well that Mrs Dixon, who was a down-to-earth, no nonsense sort of person, was deaf to all this. She was fond of Willie, very fond, though she told him off for being greedy and lazy and always getting underfoot so that she was constantly falling over him.

'It's not me that's underfoot,' Willie would grumble, 'It's you who are overdog. But I forgive you because you are so wonderful and I admire you and adore you and if you want to step on me just go right ahead and do so.'

The Dixons had got Willie when he was young from the RSPCA as an unwanted dog. Perhaps this was why Willie was so devoted to Mrs Dixon; she had thought he looked pathetic and said, 'Let's have that one.' And so it had all begun. And now Willie was, in dog terms, middle-aged, but he still thought Mrs Dixon was his mother and his rescuer and his benefactor and sang to her daily of his feelings and howled every time she went out. 'Alo-o-o-ne,' he would wail. 'She has left me alone again and I am wretched and she is cruel and she doesn't love me and I am all al-o-o-o-one.' After about five minutes he would get tired of this, find himself a nice warm comfortable place and sleep soundly till she came back again.

One Sunday the Dixons all went out to a wild-life park. Since wild-life parks do not welcome dogs Willie had to be left behind. Mrs Dixon put out a very large meal for him so that there would be no question of him getting hungry if they were late back. Willie watched her do this with an expression of abject misery that said, quite distinctly, that he thought her unfeeling and insensitive to imagine for a moment that he would be able to eat a thing, deserted and abandoned and unloved. Mrs Dixon told him briskly that he'd be fine. The Dixons left the house, locked the door, got into the car and drove off. Willie howled for exactly five minutes, then stopped, found that he was actually feeling a little peckish after all, went to his bowl and wolfed down half a tin of dog food and a handful of biscuits in thirty seconds flat.

'Creep!' said Sam, the father of the mouse family whose home was at the bottom of a box of old newspapers under the stairs. He had come out for a quick day-time forage around the kitchen.

'Mind your own business!' snarled Willie. He felt comfortably sleepy now, after that extra large meal, and was wondering where to curl up and have a good long snooze. The door to the sitting room was shut, which was a nuisance – he was specially fond of the sofa.

Sam whisked up onto the dresser, discovered that Mrs Dixon had left out the packet of dog biscuits, nipped inside and helped himself to one. 'Your trouble,' he continued, with his mouth full of biscuit, 'is that you've no sense of get up and go. No push. No oomph and zoom. You just hang about – wait for it to happen . . .'

'Leave those biscuits alone,' spluttered Willie.

'No way,' said Sam. 'Proves my point. All things come to them as helps themselves. Now me, I go out and look for it.'

 Willie glared. 'Belt up, can't you.'

Sam shrugged. 'Now if you spoke nicely to me I might see my way to chucking you down an extra biscuit.'

But Willie was no longer hungry. He was extremely full and very sleepy. He couldn't be bothered to quarrel with Sam any more. He pottered out of the kitchen and up the stairs, in search of a good sleeping place. He looked in the children's room, which was a muddle of toys and did not interest him. The bathroom was boring also. But then he discovered to his joy the Dixons' bedroom door had been left not properly closed. He gave it a good shove with his nose and went in. Oh, wonderful! If there was one place in the house that Willie preferred above all it was Mr and Mrs Dixon's bed; it was the one place, also, that was absolutely forbidden. But here he was, all alone, no one would discover him – as soon as he heard them coming back he could dash down the stairs and go through the welcome home routine as hard as he could. No one would know where he had been.

He jumped up on the bed and shuffled around a bit to make himself a nice nest. Then it occurred to him that he could do better than that. He scrabbled at the cover, got his nose underneath, heaved up the sheet and blankets and wriggled right down to the bottom of the bed. It was dark, private, and smelled gloriously of Mrs Dixon. It was paradise. Dogs, long ago and far back in their ancestries, were den animals, which is why they still like creeping under the furniture and into cosy, hidden places.

Willie had found the perfect den. He gave a great sigh of contentment and sank into a deep, deep sleep.

Towards the end of the afternoon the Dixons returned. Willie, buried in the bottom of the bed, heard nothing. He was still sleeping off that extra large meal. He slept and slept.

The Dixons searched for Willie. They searched the whole house. Mrs Dixon popped her head round the bedroom door, saw that the bed was a little untidy but thought that the children had been jumping on it. She came downstairs again and an almighty argument broke out between Mr and Mrs Dixon as to whether or not Mr Dixon had seen to it that Willie was back inside the house before they left.

'You knew I was busy getting the picnic ready,' scolded Mrs Dixon. 'I told you to put him out in the garden for five minutes and then see he was safe in the kitchen. You must have left him outside.'

'And he's gone off and got run over,' wailed Julie Dixon.

'Or been stolen,' cried Andy Dixon.

'I tell you he was in the kitchen,' shouted their father.

'He can't have been,' snapped Mrs Dixon.

'And I tell you he was,' bawled her husband.

The argument died down, as family arguments will. Whoever had done what, Willie was no longer there, which was the important thing. The children were sent to ask all the neighbours if anyone had seen anything of him. Mr Dixon drove around in the car, looking for him. There was nothing to be seen or heard of a squarish, rather overweight rough-haired white terrier.

Mrs Dixon rang up the police, who were polite and took down details but made it clear that they could not, as she suggested, put several men on the job immediately. They did, they gently pointed out, have other things to do apart from looking for people's lost dogs. Mrs Dixon, by now, was quite distraught; she put the phone down and turned on Mr Dixon again.

The entire Dixon family were by now squabbling. Mr Dixon – poor fellow – was blamed for having left Willie outside, however much he went on insisting that he hadn't. The children kept bursting into tears as they imagined the dreadful things that must have happened. Mrs Dixon, who just felt guilty in general, was snapping at everyone. Eventually she said that they had had a long day and everyone was overtired and had better go to bed. She drove the children into the bath, scurried them through their supper and tucked them up. Then she and her husband watched the news – there were no headlines, as she felt there ought to be, about 'All police leave was cancelled in the Birmingham area this evening as the search intensified for a small white terrier named Willie . . .' At last they locked the front door, turned out the lights and went upstairs.

They undressed. Mrs Dixon used the bathroom. She came back to the bedroom and took off the bedcover. She said, 'The children have been messing about in here again – just look at the state this is in.' Mrs Dixon folded the cover, put it on the chair, kicked off her slippers and slid down into the bed.

Her feet landed on something warm and hairy. She shot backwards with a yell.

Willie crawled out from under the bedclothes, blinking and looking somewhat rumpled. He saw Mrs Dixon standing beside the bed in her nightdress, began to fling himself joyfully at her, remembered with horror that he had no business to be where he was, panicked and tried to dive under the bed, where he stuck fast.

Mr Dixon hauled him out by the back legs. The children, woken by the commotion, came rushing in. Willie rolled over on his back and cringed at everyone, rolling his eyes till the whites showed. 'Don't beat me,' he begged. 'Don't murder me. It was all a ghastly mistake. I didn't mean to. I swear I never will again. If you weren't so cruel and horrible, leaving me all on my own without a bite to eat and those blessed mice making fun of me, it would never have happened.'

Willie wasn't beaten. Some stern words were said, especially by Mr Dixon. Willie was marched smartly downstairs and put to bed in the kitchen. He never got into the Dixons' bed again; not, I'm afraid, because he had learned a lesson but because Mrs Dixon took special care not to leave the door of the bedroom open.

The Mice, the Teapot and the Ball of String

THERE were three different families of mice at Fifty-four Pavilion Road. One lived in the back of the airing cupboard, another under the sitting room floorboards and a third in the bottom of a box of old newspapers under the stairs. They were all related – cousins and sisters-in-law and aunts and grand-mothers – but each family returned to its own nest by day. At night, though, everyone hunted for food throughout the house, collecting all the bits and pieces people never miss: the cornflakes under the baby's chair, the crumbs in the toaster, the scraps of fat stuck to the cooker. They exchanged news and gossip, swopped a scrap of bacon rind for a shred of baked potato skin or sat by the kitchen boiler warming themselves and nagging the children.

Young mice are brought up with rules and warn-ings which are drummed into them from the moment they leave the nest. The rules are added to or altered according to the times, but by and large have been passed on from generation to generation. They go something like this:

DON'T SLEEP IN THE DIRTY CLOTHES BASKET

DON'T TEASE THE DOG

NEVER EAT MATCHES

BE PLEASANT TO BABIES

DON'T GET INTO THE BACK OF THE TELEVISION: GREAT-UNCLE THOMAS DID THAT AND WISHED HE HADN'T

DON'T FOOL AROUND WITH EMPTY MILK BOTTLES; YOU MAY FALL IN

OVENS ARE FOR COOKING: COOKED MOUSE IS UNCOMFORTABLE

YOUR PARENTS ARE ALWAYS RIGHT

And young mice, just like human children, turn a deaf ear to a good deal of this and occasionally regret it (like great-uncle Thomas, who was a teenager at the time). Teasing the dog, indeed, was a long-standing tradition, as was a game called Scooter which involved racing each other round the lavatory seat – more dangerous by far than any milk bottle. All young mice dared one another to climb to the top of the sitting room curtains; all of them, at one time or another, explored the oven and the inside of the vacuum cleaner and slid down the big lampshade behind the sofa. They fought to be first into the toaster each night, where there was a lovely harvest of crumbs for those small enough to squeeze between the wires and swing hand over hand down to the shiny tray at the bottom. In the early mornings they played chicken in the bedroom waste-paper basket – hiding in the bottom until the very moment the Dixons started to wake up; those who were rash and stayed too long had to huddle there under kleenex and hair-combings while the floor shook as the Dixons tramped terrifyingly above and around them.

Each mouse family had tales of adventure and daring. Some of these, over the years, had become rather highly coloured. There was the ancestor who was said to have used a handkerchief to parachute from the landing down into the hall. The airing cupboard mice had a legend of a member of their family who was imprisoned in a biscuit tin when someone put the lid on while he was inside it; he ate a pound of Tea-time Fancies over the next five days and sprang out three sizes bigger when the lid was taken off again.

No doubt there was some truth in these stories, but mice, like humans, like to spin a good yarn and some of them, undoubtedly, had become a little wild. Mother mice liked to threaten their children with accounts of disaster: the young mouse who had fallen into the goldfish bowl and been gobbled up; another who drank blackcurrant syrup and turned pink; the youngest child who fell asleep inside the sewing-machine and was hemmed into a curtain.

All such stories start somewhere; most of these were lost in times past – they had happened 'Back when I was a girl . . .' or 'When my grandmother was alive . . .' or 'More years ago than I care to think . . .' But presumably all had their beginnings in some real event. Such, perhaps, as the drama of the teapot, which took place precisely as I shall tell it.

It was a night like any other. The Dixon family went to bed; Mr Dixon turned off the bedside light; downstairs the television was silent, the gas fire in the sitting room ticked from time to time as it grew cold, the light from the street-lamp splashed through the window onto the floor.

The Stair mice were first into the kitchen. The father, Sam by name and a decent enough fellow though a bit of a loud-mouth in the opinion of some, sent his children into the toaster and shinned up a chair-back onto the kitchen table, where Mrs Dixon, as usual, had left breakfast already laid. The cereal packet was an unopened one, so there was nothing doing there (he could, of course, have nibbled a hole in the corner as easy as winking, but sensible mice do not leave traces so obvious as to invite a whole programme of traps and cats). He pottered around for a while, shouted instructions to his wife, who was dealing with an apple-core one of the Dixon children had dropped behind the rubbish-bin, and greeted various friends and relations who were now appearing from the rest of the house.

The Airing Cupboard mice had some interesting gossip and the Sitting Room mice were complaining that Mr Dixon had had Sportsnight on the telly turned up full blast right above their nest under the floorboards. 'My head's splitting!' wailed the mother. 'The Grand National crashing round and round over my head . . .'

Sam's attention strayed to the teapot. Mrs Dixon had left the lid off, which was unusual. She was also in the habit of putting the tea in the pot the night before, all ready to brew up first thing in the morning. Sam was particularly fond of tea, which mice will chew much like humans at one time used to chew tobacco. He swarmed up the teapot by way of the handle and looked inside; yes, a nice little mound of Typhoo. He dropped down on top of it.

Upstairs, Mrs Dixon was lying awake. The longer she lay awake the more she had a nasty feeling she'd left the gas-fire on. The nasty feeling turned into an even nastier one that she could smell burning. She tried nudging her husband, who was comfortably snoring. At last she sighed, got out of bed, put on her dressing-gown and slippers and crept downstairs.

The mice, at the first sound of the bedroom door opening, shot between cracks in the floorboards, under the cooker and behind the sink. Sam scrabbled for a moment at the slippery sides of the teapot and decided to stay where he was.

Mrs Dixon went into the sitting room, saw the fire was off, sniffed around, came into the kitchen, put the light on, and noted that all was well. She picked up an apple core that was lying in the middle of the floor and popped it in the bin; glancing at the table, she noticed that the lid was off the teapot and put it on. Then she turned out the light, went upstairs and back to bed where she fell asleep within a few minutes.

The mice came out again. Sam's wife, Doris, called her children out from the toaster, where they had remained in hiding, counted them, and then searched unsuccessfully for her apple-core. After a few minutes it occurred to her that she didn't know where her husband was – and then suddenly all the mice became aware of Sam's faint cries coming from within the teapot.

Everyone swarmed up onto the table. They stood around the teapot and from within Sam's cries became a positive roar of distress. 'Keep calm, dear,' cried his wife. 'Take deep breaths and keep absolutely calm.' I think I should not record Sam's reply to this.

'Well,' said the oldest mouse of all, a grandfather who claimed to remember the occasion of great-uncle Thomas and the television. 'This is a nice how-d'you do.'

'Get out through the spout, father,' advised one of Sam's children, who was almost small enough to do so. Sam's reply to this cannot be repeated either.

Sam's mother, who did not often get the chance to criticize him nowadays, said that he should have known better in the first place, teapots were always unreliable and Sam had been a greedy fellow since he was so high and if she'd told him once she'd told him a thousand times – chew tea and your teeth'll drop out.

'Shut up!' bawled Sam from within the teapot.

'And don't you talk to me like that,' said his mother.

'Just keep quite calm!' wailed his wife.

The mice crowded around the teapot. What on earth was to be done? The teapot was enormous; it towered over them, its curving slippery sides decorated with a pattern of green leaves, its rim chipped where a young Dixon had once knocked it over. The mice considered what would happen in the morning. Mrs Dixon would come down, she would put the kettle on, the kettle would come to the boil, she would take the lid off the teapot, pick up the kettle and . . .

'Oh, poor father!' cried the children.

'Get me out of here!' howled Sam, not calm at all.

It was the chip in the rim of the teapot that gave them the idea. Someone pointed out that if only they could push it over, the lid would fall off . . . But of course it was far too heavy for them to push over, even everyone heaving and shoving together. If on the other hand they could tip it off the edge of the table . . . And at that moment one of them spotted the ball of string with which Mr Dixon had been tying up a parcel the night before and had left lying on the dresser – and the idea was born.

It could be done. Possibly. The thing to do was to chew off a length of string, thread it through the handle of the teapot, hang the string down over the edge of the table onto the floor, get everyone down there and then all pull, as in a tug of war.

They explained to Sam. Either the teapot would break or the lid would roll off.

Sam was silent for a moment. 'What about me?' he demanded.

'You jump out, dear,' said his wife.

'Of course I jump out,' snapped Sam. 'S'pose I've been broken too?'

It would be like flying, they told him, only quicker. It would be quite an experience. The children said they wished it was them.

Sam, within the teapot, sat on the pile of tea (one thing was for sure – he'd never chew a tea-leaf again, never in his life) and looked miserably at the curving walls of his prison. He had a sinking feeling inside him already. 'All right,' he muttered, 'get on with it.'

The other mice hardly heard him. They were already busy. One party climbed up the dresser, unreeled a length of string, bit it off and trailed it up onto the table. They passed one end through the handle of the teapot and then let the two ends fall to the ground. Then all the mice gathered on the floor and pulled both ends of the string at once. The teapot shifted slightly and Sam gave a nervous squeak. 'Watch it! I'm not ready!'

'Have you out of there in a jiffy, mate,' cried his friends.

'Hang on a minute,' pleaded Sam.

'What's the problem?'

'No problem,' said Sam. 'No hurry either. Just take it easy.'

'What's the matter, dear?' enquired his wife.

'Nothing's the matter,' snarled Sam. 'I'm having a rest, aren't I?'

'Father's afraid,' said his youngest child.

'No, I'm not,' snapped Sam. 'Another word from you and I'll belt you when I get out.'

'Father *is* afraid,' said the youngest child, more quietly.

But the mice were by now quite carried away by their cleverness and skill. Everyone was crowded around the two ends of string, ready to pull. The father of the Sitting Room mice appointed himself leader: 'When I shout HEAVE! – everyone start pulling. You all set, Sam?'

'Hold on a minute!' cried Sam, from the teapot: – 'Just want to have a few minutes to . . .'

But no one heard him. 'HEAVE!' cried the leader. They all braced themselves against the kitchen floor, from largest to smallest, and pulled for all they were worth. One or two of the smallest and youngest lost their footing, fell over backwards and hastily scrambled up again. The teapot rocked.

'Help!' cried Sam. 'Look here – I've changed my mind. I reckon I'll just stop here. Maybe if we . . .'

But his words were lost. 'HEAVE!' roared the leader again. The mice strained and heaved. The teapot lurched. 'Here we go!' cried the leader.

'Here you come, Sam! Mind your heads everyone!'

The teapot tottered and tipped. 'NO!' shrieked Sam. 'Hold it, you lot . . . Stop!'

But it was too late. He felt the teapot go over onto one side; he slid this way and that; tea showered all over him. And then his stomach was somewhere way over his head, in fact he had left it behind altogether, he was falling down . . . down . . . down . . until WHAM! . . . his prison flew apart and there he was sitting on the kitchen floor, juddering all over and with his ears ringing. And all round him were his family, friends and relations, most of them upside down, having fallen on their backs when the string slackened and the teapot came hurtling off the table.

The teapot was no more. At least it was in half a dozen pieces. And there was the most appalling noise going on; Willie the dog had been woken by the crash, had leapt out of his basket and was barking fit to burst. 'Burglars!' he yelled. 'Masked men! Raiders! Red alert!' The mice picked themselves up and began to scurry for cover. Willie caught sight of them, realised his mistake and went on barking since it now seemed the only thing to do.

The bedroom door opened. Mr Dixon came thundering downstairs. The baby woke up and started to cry. Mrs Dixon rushed to the baby. The Dixon children came padding down after their father, hoping for thrills.

Mr Dixon switched on the kitchen light. There stood Willie, still barking frantically, and there on the floor was the broken teapot. Mr Dixon swore at Willie and advanced on him with raised hand.

'I didn't do it,' whined Willie. He laid his ears back and crawled on his belly towards Mr Dixon. 'Honest. Cross my heart. It was those blessed mice, and just wait till I get my paws on one of them, I'll give them what for, I'll teach them a lesson.' But a fine lot of good that did him, since of course Mr Dixon couldn't understand a word.

The Dixon children, seeing their father about to start walloping the dog, rushed forward pleading for mercy. Mr Dixon gave Willie a few token clouts and fetched a dustpan and brush to sweep up the broken teapot. The children were sent back to bed. Mrs Dixon appeared, holding the baby, who was still howling, and wanted to know what was going on.

The baby looked over his mother's shoulder and saw Sam, who was hiding under a fold in the rug. Sam was feeling extremely dizzy and every bone in his body ached. The baby stopped crying and smiled. Sam waggled his whiskers at it. The baby smiled more and flapped his hands at Sam.

'Ssh!' said Sam. 'Not a word, eh! You be a good lad and one of these days I'll tell you a story about how I went flying in a teapot. Right?' And the baby gurgled and smiled and presently Mr and Mrs Dixon turned the kitchen light out, closed the door and went upstairs to bed again.

'Right,' snarled Willie, 'now let's be having yer . . .'

But the mice had gone, even Sam. They had slipped off to their nests by the highways and byways that only they knew about, the back alleys of a house that human beings know nothing of – the cracks and crannies and spaces below floorboards and behind skirting boards. And Sam was already forgetting his aches and pains and starting to put the polish on what was going to be a famous family story of courage and daring, in which he, of course, was the hero.

Nat and the Great Bath Climb

THE life of a young wood-louse is a very different matter to that of a young mouse. Mice are free and easy creatures compared to wood-lice. Young mice are warned and scolded, but they also get away with a good deal, since their parents are skittish creatures themselves who enjoy a bit of fun and like to get the best out of life. Wood-lice are another matter; their way of life is as stiff and awkward as their appearance. They have an outlook on life which is all their own – as indeed do most of us, but people tend to ignore that in the case of something with a top view like a very small armadillo and fourteen legs, which is why Mrs Dixon was so silly as to scream whenever she saw one. The wood-lice had to put up with a great deal more from Mrs Dixon – and the rest of the Dixons – than she did from them.

The wood-lice at Fifty-four Pavilion Road lived in several large colonies. They preferred damp and murky places – the corner behind the sink where a dripping tap had made an area of moist and flaking plaster, the cupboard in the cloakroom where mildew grew on the Dixons' winter boots, the waste-pipe of the bath.

The waste-pipe was considered a particularly attractive habitat. Admittedly two or three times each day a Niagara falls of soapy water came hurtling down and many a wood-louse had hurtled down with it and had to climb up again some fifteen feet from the drain outside. But wood-lice are sturdy uncomplaining creatures and they took this as part of the price one had to pay for a home that was forever dark, forever damp and forever undisturbed by mops and vacuum-cleaners. The waste-pipe had in fact several cracks and faulty joins through which they could climb out into the wall when threatened by bathwater. More than that, it gave them a magnificent opportunity to do what wood-lice do.

Wood-lice colonies are governed by Chief Wood-lice, who are stern and ancient creatures with whiskers of immense length. Young wood-lice are kept under the most strict control by their elders; indeed they are quite literally trampled on until large enough to hold their own. Wood-lice are not creatures who go in much for expressing themselves or being original or striking out; one wood-louse acts and thinks much like another and this is the way the old wood-lice want to keep it.

From time to time the Chief Wood-louse would call the whole colony together for a meeting. The object of this meeting was for the Chief Wood-louse to lecture the newest generation of young wood-lice, who were allowed to attend as soon as their whiskers were three millimetres long, which meant they were grown-up.

The hero of this story, who was called Nat, came to his first such meeting when he was three weeks old – which in human terms is about eighteen years. The young wood-lice sat in a row in the front, feeling important but nervous, while their parents and aunts and uncles crowded behind them and the Chief Wood-louse took up a position in front.

The Chief Wood-louse looked sternly down at the assembled crowd and began to speak. 'We are gathered together today,' he said, 'to remind ourselves of the purpose of life.' He glared at the young wood-lice. 'And what is the purpose of life?' The young wood-lice, who knew they were not supposed to answer, gazed at him respectfully.

'The purpose of life is to climb up the side of the bath. That is what we are here for. That is why we were born. No one has ever succeeded. But the purpose of life is to try. Each and every one of us. Your turn has now come. Your mothers and fathers have tried before you. Some brave spirits have tried several times. All have failed.'

There was a silence. The young wood-lice gazed at the Chief Wood-louse and felt even more nervous and important. All except Nat, who was the youngest and smallest and had been in trouble most of his life for asking too many questions. Nat was thinking.

'You will make your attempts turn and turn about, starting with the eldest. Each of you will fail, but will have made a glorious attempt, you will then have your names inscribed on the Roll of Honour.'

The young wood-lice went quite pink with pride and excitement, all except Nat, who raised one of his fourteen legs. 'Please, sir,' he said, 'why do we have to climb up the side of the bath?'

There was a gasp of horror from the crowd of woodlice. Nat's mother fainted clean away; his father bent his head in shame.

The Chief Wood-louse stared at Nat. His whiskers twitched in fury. 'WHAT DID YOU SAY?'

Nat cleared his throat and repeated, politely and clearly, 'Why do we have to climb up the side of the bath?'

The Chief Wood-louse huffed and puffed; his little black eyes bulged; he creaked with indignation.

 'BECAUSE IT'S THERE!' he roared and there

was a rustle of agreement from the crowd of wood-lice. Some of the youngsters turned to look reprovingly at Nat. His mother recovered from her faint and moaned that she would never get over the disgrace, never.

Nat sat tight. He said nothing more. He kept his thoughts to himself.

The young wood-lice made their assaults upon the side of the bath alone. Each in turn would struggle up through the plug-hole and vanish from sight. Some while later – much later, sometimes – they would crawl back down again in a state of exhaustion. One or two said with shy pride that they had got six inches before they fell back. The unluckiest of all did not crawl back into the plug-hole but tumbled back in a torrent of water, having been spotted by Mrs Dixon. One after another they tried, and one after another they returned, beaten but content. When it came to Nat's turn his parents and relatives gathered round him and told him severely that this was his chance to make a man of himself and become exactly like everyone else. 'Try hard,' they told him, 'and fail magnificently, and we shall be proud of you.'

Nat looked upwards. Bright light, which hurt his eyes, came through the plug-hole. He hauled himself up and out. It was dazzlingly bright out there and, for a few moments, he could see nothing but the glitter of the chrome circle on which he was standing. He felt terrifyingly exposed. Then he looked round and saw the whole immense smooth white length of the bath reaching away before him. It was even more enormous than people had said – it seemed to go on for ever, and if he looked to right or to left its sides towered upwards, first sloping and then absolutely sheer, up and up as far as you could see.

Nat walked out a few steps. It was very slippery. Even on the flat his legs slithered about. He toiled across to one side and gradually the smooth hard surface began to slope. He slithered even more. He slithered back to where he had started.

He looked at those white cliffs. Of course you couldn't climb them. That was the whole point.

He struggled a little way up the slope again. Then he lost his grip and rolled down to the bottom.

Stuff this, thought Nat, I'm not carrying on with this lark. He sat down where he was and looked around him. The bath was a very boring place, he decided – either flat white or steep white and with nothing to look at. There was one of Mr Dixon's hairs, which to Nat was like a length of rope but not very interesting. There was also a grain of Mrs

Dixon's bath-salts which he tried to eat; it tasted nasty so he spat it out. He thought about going back down the plug-hole; he could say – truthfully enough – that he had tried to climb up the side of the bath, and failed. He could have his name inscribed on the Roll of Honour, like everyone else. The idea of that was as boring as the scenery of the bath.

'Well!' said a voice. 'Get on with it, then! Strive and struggle! Press on! Wear yourself out! That's what you're here for, isn't it?'

Nat looked all round. He could see no one.

'What's the matter?' continued the voice. 'Where's your grit and determination?'

Nat looked up. Far above him, on the distant heights of the right hand side of the bath, he saw some legs. The legs twitched, took a few neat steps downwards and a large spider came into view.

'Go on,' said the spider, 'climb. Give me something to laugh at.'

'I'm not going to,' said Nat. 'There's no point. We can't.'

The spider let out a length of thread and swung itself down until it was hanging halfway down the side of the bath. 'Good grief! The first one of you with his head screwed on right. Too right you can't.

I, on the other hand . . .' It gripped the side of the bath for a moment, and then swarmed up its thread and re-appeared at the top. 'Neat, eh?'

'Terrific,' said Nat. 'What is it like up there?'

'Truth to tell,' said the spider, 'there's not all that much to it. Quite a nice view. Come and see.'

Nat stared. 'But . . .' he began.

'Wait,' ordered the spider. It raised its two rear legs and began to spin a great length of thread, which streamed out and came floating down until the end of it reached Nat in the bottom of the bath. 'Take hold,' instructed the spider. 'Hang on tight.'

Nat gripped the thread, which was sticky and felt slightly elastic but strong. The spider became very busy with its eight legs and Nat felt himself being slowly towed up the slope of the bath. He clung on for dear life. The spider continued to reel in the thread and Nat found himself rising up the sheer white wall. He swung around alarmingly and once or twice was bumped against the side. 'Fend off,' advised the spider. 'Use your feet. Not much further.'

Up went Nat. He did not dare look down. Once, he thought; I am doing what no other wood-louse has ever done.

'There!' said the spider. 'Piece of cake, isn't it?'

Nat found himself standing on a white cliff-top.

He walked to the far edge and looked out into the bathroom, which, since wood-lice are better at smelling than seeing, appeared to him as a dizzying scene of distant and colourful blurs. There was a terrifying drop down to a great expanse of green (which was in fact the bathmat) and an overwhelming smell of flowers (which came from Mrs Dixon's Country Garden talcum powder). I am where no other wood-louse has ever been, thought Nat.

'Mind,' said the spider, 'once you're here there's not a lot to do. One just kind of hangs out for a bit and then goes down again. Personally I find the top of the standard lamp in the sitting room more exhilarating. But you wouldn't know about that.'

'No,' said Nat. He didn't think he wanted to either.

'Anyway, you'll have something to tell the folks back home.'

'No,' said Nat. 'I can't possibly tell them. This isn't the way you're supposed to do it.'

'Well, suit yourself.' The spider began grooming itself with its two front legs. Nat noticed that on one side it had two legs that were very much shorter than the others.

'What happened to your legs?' he asked. He had

often seen spiders before but had never been on such close terms with one and, as we know, he was fond of asking questions.

'Nosy fellow, aren't you?' said the spider. 'I had a slight difference of opinion with a friend, as it happens. Quite good fun at the time.' It was a ferocious looking creature; you'd do well to stay on the right side of it, Nat thought.

'How about a quick spin down to the bathmat and up to the laundry basket?' continued the spider.

Nat thanked it but said he thought he ought to be getting back now. The spider spun a short length of thread, Nat took hold of it, and the spider lowered him slowly over the side and down into the bath again. When he got to the bottom Nat gave the thread a tug, as he had been instructed, let go of it, and the spider reeled it back in again. Then it peered down over the edge and called, 'Well, cheerio then. See you around, I daresay.'

'Cheerio,' called Nat, 'and thanks very much. I enjoyed it.'

'Don't mention it,' said the spider. 'Take care. Don't do anything I wouldn't do.'

Nat trudged back down the length of the bath. He slithered across the chrome of the plug-hole and down into the dark, homely hole. He crawled down the damp, familiar pipe and when he got to the first bend there was a reception committee of wood-lice waiting for him, headed by the Chief Wood-louse.

'You have tried to climb up the side of the bath?' said the Chief Wood-louse, in his most stern and dreadful tones.

'Yes, sir,' said Nat.

'And you have failed?'

'Yes, sir,' said Nat.

'Then,' said the Chief Wood-louse 'I shall inscribe your name on the Roll of Honour. From now on you are exactly the same as every other wood-louse. Be proud of it.'

'Yes, sir,' said Nat.

And being a sensible fellow, he kept to himself for ever after the fact that he had been where no wood-louse had ever been before.

Sam and the Honda Ride

SAM was restless. He would grumble to his family and friends about how bored he was, and how he never got a chance to try anything new and he was wasted stuck here at Pavilion Road day in day out. He would stare out of the windows. 'Out there,' he would say, 'a mouse could breathe.'

His wife, who had heard all this before, would snap, 'Don't be silly, dear. You'd get lost in two minutes. Or the cat would have you.' Sam's children would egg him on. 'Go on, Dad,' they would say, 'dare you! Go out there!' And Sam would slip under the back door and saunter around for a while on the back doorstep, or even get as far as the edge of the back lawn, before he lost his nerve and came bolting back; 'Got something in my eye,' he would say, 'Couldn't see where I was going any more . . .' or 'Starting to rain. Better leave it till tomorrow.'

For Sam was not quite the bold fellow he made himself out to be. Truth to tell the outside world scared him stiff – though it also fascinated him. He really did want to go out there and explore; but at the same time he was terrified of the idea. This mixture of feelings boiled away within him in the most uncomfortable way. He would force himself to venture out and then a noise or a shadow would set his heart thumping and he would scuttle back, furious with himself.

But one night he discovered the garage. The Dixons' garage was close up beside the house and the first time Sam went in there he did so by mistake. He had not meant to go further than a few feet from the front door (he had wriggled through a gap in the draught excluder). He was scrounging inside a Mars bar wrapper dropped by one of the children when a sudden rustle sent him into a panic and he shot under the door of the garage, imagining every cat in the street on his tail.

Inside there was an enormous shiny monster, but Sam could see at once that it was dead so he paid it no attention and lurked cautiously by the wall until he was sure there were no further dangers. As well as the Dixons' car there was the lawnmower, a clutter of pots of paint and garden tools, and another, smaller and equally dead monster which was in fact a Honda motorbike. The Honda belonged to the Dixons' next door neighbour's son, Kevin, who was eighteen and worked at a factory a few miles away. Kevin used the motorbike to go to and from work, as well as to meet his friends in the evenings, and the Dixons allowed him to keep it in their garage. The Honda was Kevin's pride and joy: it sat there gleaming in the darkness, a blaze of silver and shiny black. Sam stared at it.

He crept across the oily floor, feeling very brave, and sniffed around it. Clearly, it was quite harmless. It smelled of petrol and polish but there was also another, more interesting smell coming from somewhere up above him. The smell of bacon-flavoured crisps. Now, if there was one thing Sam would go to any lengths to get, it was a bacon-flavoured crisp. He forgot all about cats and scary noises, swarmed up the side of the monster – with some difficulty since it was slippery – and sat on the saddle, sniffing frantically. Ah! The smell was coming from that deep white box behind. Sam peered over the edge – and there in the bottom was a bacon-flavoured crisp packet with at least three crisps still in it. Joy of joys! Sam slithered down into the box and started to tuck in.

Next door, Kevin was coming downstairs, yawning dreadfully and trying not to wake his parents. It was five o'clock in the morning and he was on the early shift. He let himself out of the house, put on his crash helmet, yawned some more, and rolled up the Dixons' garage door.

Sam, in the bottom of the bike carrier, eating the best bacon-flavoured crisp of his life, heard the most appalling roaring sound and froze in horror. He crept under the crisp packet and kept quite still. Heavy footsteps approached. Two more packets of crisps and a foil-wrapped ham sandwich dropped down on top of him – Kevin's breakfast. The lid was slammed on the box, which began to rock violently from side to side. Sam, within, was flung to and fro; he squeaked in terror and scrabbled at the sides of the box. Too late, much too late.

Kevin wheeled the Honda out into the road, got on and kicked the starter.

There was the most deafening noise Sam had ever heard in his life. He juddered all over from nose to tail. And then the noise settled to a steady drone and the box jiggled and shook and bounced and Sam jiggled and shook and bounced with it. It was appalling. He had never been so scared in his life. It was worse by far than the teapot adventure. He had no idea what was happening. Was he in some kind of machine?

He knew about machines because of the fridge that hummed and buzzed in the Dixons' kitchen, and Mrs Dixon's vacuum-cleaner that roared over his head when he was trying to sleep under the floorboards. But this machine, if that was what it was, seemed to have gone mad; it howled and growled and bounced – it appeared to be flying. Sam remembered all the times he had wished he could fly like the racing pigeon or the starlings. He moaned. If this was flying, he'd had enough. More than enough. And he never wanted to see another bacon-flavoured crisp in his life. Never ever. He was rolling around in bacon-flavoured crisps, down in the bottom of his thundering white prison; he stank of bacon-flavoured crisp; there were bits of bacon-flavoured crisp in his ears and clinging to his fur.

And then all of a sudden there was silence. The box ceased to bounce around; the dreadful roaring stopped.

Kevin switched off the Honda's engine and wheeled it to a place in the factory bike park. He was still yawning; the ten-minute run to work was something he did more or less in his sleep, when he was on the early shift. He opened the bike carrier, picked up his sandwich and his packets of crisps; he just missed picking up the end of Sam's tail too. He looked at his watch and saw that he was late, shoved the lid back without closing it properly, and rushed off.

Sam lay among bacon-flavoured crisps, gasping.

He felt bruised and battered all over. He stretched his legs, gingerly; nothing seemed to be broken. He looked up and saw a crack of daylight. He tried to climb the side of the box, slipped back, jumped, slipped again, jumped once more and grabbed the edge of the box with his front paws. He hauled himself up and slithered through the crack and down the outside of the box without even looking to see where he was. All he wanted was to escape from this mad flying monster.

There was a great open space, far too much of it. Sam did not like open spaces. He scurried into a clump of grass and peered out.

The bike park was a patch of waste ground some distance from the factory. It was a scruffy place with black cindery earth, withered grass, a few bushes and much litter by way of tins and bottles and rotting newspapers. Nearby was a high wire fence and on the other side of the fence was the factory's rubbish tip. Sam, of course, did not know all this; he looked out of his sparse shelter, saw the row of sparkling motorbikes, a Coke tin and a flapping copy of *The Sun* and thought this was the most horrible place on earth. He could feel wide high sky above him, which was terrifying, and could smell horrid and unfamiliar smells: smoke, exhaust fumes and disagreeable rubbish. He was too miserable to do anything but sit there, quivering.

All of a sudden he felt a great shadow come swooping down above him. Even a mouse that has led a sheltered life in a house has instincts about swooping shadows. Sam shot sideways out of the clump of grass and under a rusty petrol can. The great yellow beak of the seagull missed him by inches; the bird flapped away, squawking angrily. Sam, almost fainting, crouched under the petrol tin.

'You want to watch out for them,' said a voice. 'Nasty beggars. Not that they bother me a lot – they know I'll give as good as I get.'

A large whiskered face was staring at him through the fence. Sam had never seen a rat before; Pavilion Road had many inhabitants but they did not include rats.

'Stopping here long?' enquired the rat. 'There's good pickings, I can tell you.' Sam shuddered. He looked beyond the rat towards the rubbish tip, which was a smoking waste-land that stank of decay. For a mouse accustomed to the best toast crumbs, it was a hideous prospect. Moreover, there was a seething mass of seagulls above it. A crow sat on a nearby post. Sam felt overcome with despair. He closed his eyes and gave a low moan.

'You look a bit off colour, mate,' said the rat cheerfully. 'Here, have a bit of this – it'll perk you up.'

Sam opened his eyes and found a large chunk of mouldy raw bacon under his nose. It made him feel even worse, if possible. But it was kindly meant, evidently this rat was a decent enough fellow, and it wouldn't do to offend him. Sam pulled himself together and explained that he wasn't hungry, and that he was here by accident and wanted only to get away again. Though, he added hastily, he was sure it was a fine place if you were used it.

'How come you're here anyway?' enquired the rat.

'I flew,' said Sam, shuddering at the memory.

'Stupid . . . That's for birds.' The rat began to eat the mouldy bacon. 'Anyway, while you're here you want to have a look round. Best tip in town, this is. Rotten potatoes, mattresses, old TV sets – you name it, we've got it. The other day a bloke brought a whole load of burnt chips. Wow! Did we have a blow-out!'

Sam came out from under the petrol can, with a cautious glance skywards.

'Come on,' said the rat, 'I'll give you a tour of the best stuff.'

Sam followed him through the wire fence and out

into a world of hills and valleys and sudden terrible craters, a world that flapped and stank, that even smoked in places. There were great heaps of old clothes and heaving plastic, valleys of ash and cinders, horrid holes filled with smelly oily water. There were fridges without doors and rusty cookers, old shoes and prams and lawn mowers. The rat had his home in an upside-down sofa, a fine mansion of springs and foam rubber, most impressive. It smelled, though, of mould, damp and bad fish. The rat was not a fussy housekeeper. Sam's whiskers twitched as he picked his way among fish-bones and other leavings. He thought of Pavilion Road with its clean floors and smells of polish, soap and toast. Tears came into his eyes.

'Sit down,' said the rat. 'Make yourself at home.'

And then from somewhere above and beyond there came a tremendous grinding and whooshing noise. The rat leapt up.

'Oops!' he cried. 'Fresh supplies! Let's get going!'

Sam hurried after him out into the rubbish tip again; it seemed better to stick to the only friend he had in this awful place. He was just in time to see a monstrous yellow machine fling a shower of rubbish on top of all that was already there. Immediately the sky was full of seagulls, squawking and squabbling;

Sam, cowering under a plastic bag, could see glaring yellow eyes, snapping bills and great claws. The rat, apparently unworried, dashed out, dug around and returned with a banana skin. Had Sam come upon this at Pavilion Road he would have considered it quite a find, but as it was all he could do was mutter again that he wasn't hungry. The rat munched the banana skin and looked thoughtfully at Sam. 'You're a funny bloke . . . You don't eat. You jump out of your skin every two seconds. What's wrong?'

'I want to go home,' said Sam dolefully.

The rat finished the banana skin and started on a cabbage leaf. '*How* did you say you got here?'

Sam explained. Rather more precisely this time: the fearful shiny machine that roared and flew; the white box.

'Oh!' exclaimed the rat. 'One of *those* . . . I'm with you now. Well, you'll have to go back the same way, won't you?'

He plunged off into the tip once more, past bicycle wheels and old tyres and mounds of detergent bottles, with Sam panting behind. When they got to the wire fence again the rat waved a paw. 'There you are,' he said, 'which one?'

Sam looked. There, not far away, was a whole row of shiny machines – dozens of them, all of them, so far as he could see, exactly alike. Most of them had a white box at the back. The flicker of hope that he had felt died down. He looked hopelessly at the rat.

'Why did you get in there in the first place?' asked the rat, with a touch of impatience.

'Bacon-flavoured crisps!' cried Sam, inspired. 'That's it! It'll be the one that smells of bacon-flavoured crisps. That was why I got into the box.'

'Ah!' said the rat. 'Now you're talking. Let's get going, then.'

He scuttled over to the machines and began to sniff his way along the row. Chip butties . . . chicken leg . . . Mars Bar . . . Ah! What about this, then?'

And as he spoke he swarmed up the back wheel of one of the machines. From the seat he peered down at Sam. 'Are you getting any sort of bacon-flavoured crisp pong down there?'

'Yes, I am!' cried Sam excitedly.

'Come on up,' instructed the rat.

Sam scrambled up. And they both saw, now, that the lid of the white box was slightly open. And from within there came, indeed, a fine and reassuring smell of bacon-flavoured crisp.

'Well,' said the rat, 'you're in luck. Cheerio, then.'

Sam said good-bye warmly and thanked him for his trouble. The rat vanished and Sam slithered down inside the white box and crept underneath the empty crisp packet. He was trembling now at the thought of another of those dreadful journeys. His ordeal was by no means over. But by now he was exhausted. He closed his eyes, sighed, and fell fast asleep.

He woke with a start to find the box shuddering and the machine roaring. At first he thought he was in a nightmare and then it all came back. He clung onto the crisp packet and settled down, grimly, to wait for it to be over. Which, after a hideous interval, it was. The machine ceased to fly, the roaring became a grumble and ceased altogether. Sam braced himself; he knew what he had to do if he was to escape.

The lid of the box was lifted and at the same moment Sam leapt out. Kevin gave a yelp of surprise as Sam dashed up his sleeve, sprang on to the garage floor and shot behind some old sacks. For the next couple of days Kevin would be telling anyone who would listen a tale about how a mouse had jumped out of his bike carrier, which of course no one believed.

Sam waited until he had gone, and then crept out and back into Fifty-four Pavilion Road. He slipped into a familiar back alley that ran behind the kitchen wainscot to his home under the stairs, where his family were having a mid-day snooze.

'There you are, dear,' said his wife, 'we were just wondering. Where've you been, then?'

Sam took a deep breath. And then he began to talk of machines that flew, of birds the size of cushions, of a place that reached further than you could see in every direction and in which there were sights and smells that were beyond description. He grew big and bold again as he talked. He told them of his friend the rat. He was Sam the traveller, Sam the intrepid, Sam the glorious.

And his family, who had heard this kind of thing before, listened up to a point. The children whispered and fidgeted. Their mother dozed. Once, the youngest child nudged her and said, 'Ma – is Father telling the truth?' at which she woke up and said sternly, 'Your father always tells the truth,' – then dozed off again.

Nat and the Spider Battle

NAT, the wood-louse, was not quite like other wood-lice. He looked exactly like them: stiff armour-plated back, fourteen legs, small black eyes, long whiskers. Even his own mother couldn't tell him apart from the rest of her children. But he had a mind of his own, a spirit of independence – you will remember the great bath climb – and he liked to keep himself to himself. He visited, from time to time, places that other wood-lice prefer to avoid – the bedroom win-dowsill, the kitchen floor.

It was thus – prowling around under the kitchen table one day – that disaster befell him. Mrs Dixon happened to be sweeping up. Nat, trundling along without a thought in his head, found himself at-tacked from above by some immense descending cloud, hurled along the floor and tumbled with dust, crumbs and bits of paper into a red cavern (the dust-pan) and thence into a fearful, smelly pit (the waste-bin).

He unrolled himself (wood-lice, like hedgehogs, curl up when alarmed). He sighed. Well, he thought, I'll have to get meself out of here, won't I? He began to forge his way upwards through potato peelings, lettuce leaves and newspaper. After what seemed a long time he saw daylight. He ploughed onwards and came out at last through a crack onto a shiny top. This had a nasty slippery feel so he set off once more, up a wooden cliff that was quite an easy climb. This was in fact the side of the sink unit and when Nat reached the top he found himself on a shining silver plain with ridges along which he slithered uncomfortably. Don't like this place, he thought, I'll have to get away from here . . . And no sooner had he thought it than his legs slid from under him altogether and he found himself tumbling over the edge and down, down, down . . .

And splash into the washing-up bowl, which was half filled with water.

Now I've gone and done it, thought Nat. He floated on his back, his fourteen legs kicking hopelessly. He floated round and round in circles. Well, he thought, I don't see how I'm going to get out of this one. He floated in glum resignation, staring up at the distant ceiling, which he couldn't even see. So that's that, he thought.

'Having fun?'

Nat swivelled one eye, in so far as this was possible. There on the edge of the washing-up bowl was perched the spider. His friend the spider.

'No,' said Nat, 'since you ask.'

'I thought you people couldn't swim?'

'We can't,' said Nat, 'that's the problem.'

'Ah,' said the spider, 'why didn't you say so? Watch out!" And so saying, he began to shoot out a silken line which spun slowly towards Nat. 'Grab hold,' instructed the spider. 'And hang on tight.'

Nat seized the thread with as many legs as he could and clung on. He felt himself dragged across the water and then swung upwards.

The spider had vanished. 'Thanks,' cried Nat breathlessly, 'That'll do nicely. Thanks a lot . . .' But still he went spinning upwards, clinging onto the spider's silk rope, upwards and upwards, dizzyingly, the sink unit and the washing-up bowl now distant beneath him. And there was the spider again, he saw, scuttling up the window-frame at enormous speed, pausing once to let out more thread, then dashing on up.

'Hey,' called Nat, whirling round and round, going up and up. 'Hey . . . That's enough.'

But on he went, and on went the spider, vanishing again now into a crack at the corner of the window, and on went Nat until suddenly he too reached the crack, found his feet on solid ground once more and the spider grinning out at him. Help! thought Nat, *Now* where am I?'

'This is my pad,' said the spider, 'Care for some fly?'

'No, thanks,' said Nat. 'I'm a vegetarian.'

'Suit yourself. Excuse me a minute – small repair job I should see to.'

They were high up at the top of the kitchen window. Far down below were the sink and the table and the fridge and the cooker. And Willie the dog, asleep on the mat beside the boiler. The spider's web, Nat now saw, was stretched right across one corner of the window, a fine and intricate affair like a great wheel of spokes and cross-bars. There was another, smaller one the other side. The spider was bustling around some broken lines. He came back, grumbling. 'Blue-bottles. Get one of those darn things thrashing around and there's a night's work gone west. Well, how d'you like it up here?'

'Very nice,' said Nat politely. 'Fine view.' He was thinking what a long time it was going to take to crawl down again and find his way back to the nest in the back of the china cupboard, where his family was living at the moment.

'It's all mine,' said the spider, 'As far as you can see. My territory.' He waved a leg around 'The window is mine and the ceiling as far as the light fitting and behind the freezer is mine and the top shelf of the dresser.'

'I see,' said Nat. After a moment he added, 'Whose is the rest?'

The spider growled. He gnashed his teeth, up to a point and in so far as spiders have teeth. He really was a ferocious-looking fellow. 'My neighbour's,' he snarled.

Nat thought. He looked at the spider's legs, two of which were still somewhat shorter than the rest. 'Is that the one you had the argument with,' he enquired, 'that you told me about last time?'

'That's him,' snapped the spider.

'Ah,' said Nat. Spiders must be a funny lot, he thought. What was all this about territories, and chopping each other's legs off? Wood-lice, it should be said, are peaceable creatures who browse quietly in flocks with seldom a cross word, except for some rather stern discipline of the young. I dunno, thought Nat . . . Still, they say it takes all sorts to make a world.

All of a sudden the spider appeared to go crazy. He hunched himself into a black baleful knot, which somehow made him look even more fierce than before; he blew himself out until he seemed twice as large as he really was; he huffed and puffed, he growled and gnashed.

'What's the matter?' asked Nat nervously.

'There he is!' spat the spider.

Nat looked. And there on the far side of the window, he saw, was another spider. Also hunching itself and blowing itself out, glaring and snarling.

'All right . . .' roared the spider. 'If that's the way you want it . . . Here I come!'

Bless my soul, thought Nat, what a fuss . . . The spider went galloping off across the top of the window; the other spider advanced from his corner. And in the middle they met, with a horrid sound (to Nat) of clashing legs, shouts and oaths. The two spiders clutched each other round the middle like Japanese wrestlers; they swiped at each other with their back ends. Nat's friend succeeded in shoving his rival off the window altogether, but he merely dropped down a foot or so on a length of thread and then came swarming up again, back to the fray. They rampaged to and fro. The noise (to Nat) was quite terrible. It seemed extraordinary that, far below, the dog Willie should be sleeping in front of the boiler and Mrs Dixon having a cup of coffee without paying the slightest attention.

'Take that!' panted Nat's friend . . . And, 'Gotcha!' roared his neighbour.

Oh dear, thought Nat, there goes another leg! And indeed both spiders were beginning to look somewhat the worse for wear. Nat's friend was down to six legs again; the enemy had lost the whole of one and half of another two. And then all of a sudden they stopped, backed off, and the battle was apparently over.

The spider returned, out of breath. 'There!' he said. 'How did you like that? Good, wasn't it!'

'Who won?' enquired Nat.

'A draw,' said the spider. 'It always is. That way we start again level the next time.'

'What was it about?'

'About?' The spider stared irritably at Nat. 'What d'you mean – what was it about? It wasn't about anything.'

'I mean,' said Nat, 'why do you fight him?'

The spider became even more irritable. 'Because as soon as I see him I feel like fighting. In fact even talking about him makes me feel like fighting. Grr . . .' And he began to rattle his legs threateningly.

Nat thought it best to change the subject. 'I'd better be pushing off. My folks will be wondering where I've got to.'

'No need to rush,' said the spider. 'You haven't seen my larder.'

Nat wasn't at all sure that he wanted to, but it

seemed wisest to oblige so he followed the spider into his den, a crack in the window-frame leading to a hole in the wall. There, neat parcels done up in silk thread were stacked in rows. The spider contemplated them, a little gloomily. 'Mind, you can get tired of fly, day in day out. Sometimes I wonder about experimenting a bit.'

Nat backed away quickly. 'I wouldn't do that,' he said, 'my mum always says you shouldn't go against nature.'

'I daresay not,' said the spider. 'All the same, life gets tedious. One builds webs. One fights. One eats fly. What's the point of it all, I sometimes wonder.' He glared at Nat, as though it might be in some way his fault. 'Don't you?'

'No,' said Nat 'I have enough trouble with falling on my back and not being able to get right way up again.'

'You're the wrong shape,' said the spider.

Nat began to say that that was a matter of opinion, and then thought better of it. 'It's a good shape for some things,' he observed.

'Such as?'

'Getting through cracks. Going under stones.'

The spider sniffed. 'Possibly.'

'Of course,' said Nat, 'I can see it's another matter

altogether being able to make webs and drop from enormous heights on a line.'

'Right!' exclaimed the spider, brightening up.

'And fourteen legs is rather too many, whereas eight is just about right. Or six . . .' he added, with a quick glance at the spider.

'Exactly!'

'Still,' said Nat with a sigh, 'there it is. One makes the best of it. And now I really must be off.'

'Shall I give you a hand?' enquired the spider graciously.

But Nat replied that no, it was very kind but he would make his own way home. And he set off on his slow journey down the wall, trundling along at his own speed, avoiding slippery places, looking for crumbly plaster and rough wood that his fourteen legs could get a grip on. Here we go, he said to himself, steady does it, all the time in the world . . .

And as he went the life of the Dixon kitchen raged around him. The children came home from school and had their tea. Everyone talked at once. Someone spilled a bottle of milk. Mrs Dixon stepped on Willie. Nobody at all was even aware of Nat, making his slow and patient journey from the top of the window to the bottom of the china cupboard, except the baby, who spotted him working his way down the dresser and pointed and said something to which no one paid any attention. Nat waved his whiskers at the baby and continued. And when at last he reached his nest, where all his friends and relations were curled up under damp plaster behind Mrs Dixon's wedding-present vase that she never used, his mother said suspiciously, 'Where've you been, then?'

'Nowhere,' said Nat. And went to sleep.

Penguin Children's 60s

ALI BABA AND THE FORTY THIEVES • *Retold by N. J. Dawood*
THE AMAZING PIPPI LONGSTOCKING • *Astrid Lindgren*
ANNE AT GREEN GABLES • *L. M. Montgomery*
AT THE RIVER-GATES AND
OTHER SUPERNATURAL STORIES • *Philippa Pearce*
CLASSIC GHOST STORIES
CLASSIC NONSENSE VERSE
THE CLOCKWORK MOUSE • *Dick King-Smith*
DEAD MAN'S LANE • *Joan Aiken*
THE DRAGON ON THE ROOF • *Terry Jones*
FOUR GREAT GREEK MYTHS • *Roger Lancelyn Green*
THE GREAT MOUSE PLOT AND
OTHER TALES OF CHILDHOOD • *Roald Dahl*
THE GREAT TIME WARP ADVENTURE • *Jon Scieszka*
THE HOOLIGAN'S SHAMPOO • *Philip Ridley*
KEEP IT IN THE FAMILY • *Anne Fine*
KING ARTHUR'S COURT • *Roger Lancelyn Green*
THE LITTLE MERMAID AND
OTHER FAIRY TALES • *Hans Andersen (Translated by Naomi Lewis)*
LOST DOG AND OTHER STORIES • *Penelope Lively*
THE MIDNIGHT STORY • *Margaret Mahy*
MOOMINTROLLS AND FRIENDS • *Tove Jansson*
MRS PEPPERPOT TURNS DETECTIVE • *Alf Prøysen*
THE NIGHT TRAIN: STORIES IN PROSE AND VERSE • *Allan Ahlberg*
THE PIED PIPER OF HAMELIN AND OTHER CLASSIC STORIES IN VERSE
ROBIN HOOD AND HIS MERRY MEN • *Roger Lancelyn Green*
SHERLOCK HOLMES AND THE SPECKLED BAND • *Sir Arthur Conan Doyle*
SMACKING MY LIPS • *Michael Rosen*
TALES FROM ALICE IN WONDERLAND • *Lewis Carroll*
TALES FROM THE JUNGLE BOOK • *Rudyard Kipling*
THREE QUIRKY TAILS • *Paul Jennings*
TOM SAWYER'S PIRATE ADVENTURE • *Mark Twain*
TOM THUMB AND OTHER FAIRY TALES • *Jacob and Wilhelm Grimm*

Some other Puffin books by Penelope Lively

ASTERCOTE
A HOUSE INSIDE OUT
THE WHISPERING KNIGHTS